D1637428

Attachment

THE FRENCH LIST

Attachment

FLORENCE NOIVILLE

TRANSLATED BY TERESA LAVENDER FAGAN

LONDON NEW YORK CALCUTTA

All quotes by Molière are from Molière, *'The Misanthrope' and 'Tartuffe'* (Richard Wilbur trans.) (Orlando, FL: Mariner Books, 1965).

The quotes by Barthes are from Roland Barthes, *A Lover's Discourse: Fragments* (Richard Howard trans.) (London: Vintage, 2002).

Seagull Books, 2015

First published as *L'attachement* by Florence Noiville
© Editions Stock, 2012

First published in English translation by Seagull Books, 2015

English translation © Teresa Lavender Fagan, 2015

ISBN 978 0 8574 2 233 0

British Library Cataloguing-in-Publication Data
A catalogue record for this book is available from the British Library

Typeset by Seagull Books, Calcutta, India
Printed and bound at Hyam Enterprises, Calcutta, India

ACKNOWLEDGEMENTS

My thanks to Cees Nooteboom (who, in *Rituals*, tells the story of Kawabata); to Witold Gombrowicz (the advice on page 66 is a variation on 'My advice before dying,' in *Gombrowicz, un structuraliste de la rue*, by Jean-Pierre Salgas, Editions de L'Éclat, 2011); to Robert Musil; and to Molière, without whom this story might not have existed.

Thanks also to Vlaams Fonds voor de Letteren, to the Elzenveld home in Anvers and to the Passa Porta home in Brussels, whose staff were of great assistance while I was writing this book.

'Whatever is anachronic is obscene.'

Roland Barthes
A Lover's Discourse: Fragments

Marie

How many 'me's are there? Do you ask yourself that question, too? There are so many fragments, all those mismatched 'me's that look at one another without understanding. The one who speaks and the one who writes, the one who loves and the one who reasons, the one who is passionate and the one who doubts. There is someone in me who acts and someone who watches me act. The second one says to the other, 'Why did you do that? Why did you do it?'

I always ask myself that question when I think about our story, and I can't come up with an answer. That doesn't mean I regret the past, or that it doesn't haunt me. I'm like someone swimming upstream, constantly carried back. I try to look at our story but it hypnotizes me. I want to discover something in it but I don't know what. The birth of the feeling of love? The mysterious need that brings us together? By looking through a magnifying glass at that instance of insane love, a love beyond all logic and reason, I try to isolate the force. The force of attraction. What is it that makes us act when we become attracted to a person whom we should never even have spoken to?

Marie

I turned 49 this year, maybe that's why I'm writing to you. You were 49 when we met. It's strange how old you seemed to me then, my dear H., I can tell you that now. The paradox, although I was only 17 at the time, is that I also felt beyond any age. An old young person. School, degrees, marriage, children—life seemed like a tunnel that was opening up before me, sucking me in like a gaping mouth. Is that why I ran into your arms? At 17, was my mind already distorted from being too far removed from life?

I'm writing to you because I don't want to phone. I've thought a thousand times of that phone call I won't make. That I will never make. A long ringing in the emptiness, then your wife picks up. In the past, when she would answer, she would say in her unbearably sweet voice, 'Just a moment, I'll get H. . . .' This time her intonation will be different. Indifferent? She'll say, '. . . I thought . . . H. is dead . . . you didn't know . . . ?' A long silence. How could I have known? H. and I haven't seen each other for years. A few notes from time to time, on birthdays, the New Year. Brief moments of catching up that became increasingly spaced apart . . .

In our imaginary conversation your wife continues. She talks about the winter, the cold snap. She mentions the word 'coma'. She talks about your heart as if I didn't know it. She still has that sweet voice that I detest and respect at the same time. But this time I think I detect tones of revenge. She has regained her power over the fallen ex-Lolita.

Suddenly, images of your funeral surge up before me—your wife is leading the ceremony by herself. The last thing she needed was for me to be there. 'No, my dear, you have done enough to ruin my life, don't you think?'

In real life she wouldn't say that. She wouldn't say anything like that on the phone. I'm the one who would like her to explode for once with the violence she never showed—out of love, pride, dignity?

On that day, in any case, she would be the official widow, standing straight between your two sons, the *normalien* and the *polytechnicien*—they were around my age, I wonder whatever became of them.

As for her, she would have to wait for your death for everything to get back to normal.

Normal, indeed! Everyone always used that word. I can still hear my mother, 'Your relationship is not normal.'

Anna

As I drive up to the house I listen to the night sounds—
hooting, hissing, the rustling of wings. When I turn off the
car lights it is completely dark, a dark that one forgets in
the city. Groping, I open the door, and I immediately recognize the smell—a mixture of furniture polish and holi-
days. In the foyer there is a note from Suzanne who is
delighted that I'm coming to the country to study for my
medical-school exams. 'The bed is made in your mother's
room.'

I recognize the bed sheets with the intertwined initials, with the weight I love to feel on my legs. Outside, that
uncertain hooting is still going on. A cry or an omen? The
announcement of an ending or a beginning?

Marie

'Thou hast doves' eyes . . . thy lips are like a thread of scarlet
. . . thy neck is like the tower of David builded for an
armory.'

I listen to you reading the Song of Songs in the big
empty house. We're in my room, the blue room, one June
afternoon. The sun is coming in through the window,
with the sounds of the river. It brings with it the smell of
warm mud. And everything blends together in my memory, the warmth on my half-naked body, the sound of your
serious voice, the poetry of the text, the excitement of the
forbidden.

Do you remember how it all happened? I'm the one
who initiated things. Earlier, I had come to see you after
class. The *bac* was getting closer and I wanted your advice
on what prep class I should take. Advanced or not? Since I
was in your class, I had no doubt you could tell me.

I see myself alone with you in that classroom. On the
blackboard, a phrase from *Lucien Leuwen*: 'Try not to spend
your life hating and being afraid.'

I was leaning on a desk in the first row, awkward,
swinging one of my legs, and I could feel myself blushing.
There was chalk dust floating in the light.

All of the previous year I was agitated without really admitting it—later I was told that you were too, that it was obvious. That day, in any case, I had the audacity of the shy. I came to talk to you in private. And I couldn't believe it when you said, 'I've been waiting for you . . .'

I'm not pretending I was innocent, though I sincerely went to ask for your advice. But what if I also understood what was causing my agitation? Was I experiencing my power of seduction? Taking a risk? Playing with fire? Knowing that you represented an escape route from the tunnel that was sucking me in?

Young girls should never be allowed to play with matches.

I remember the dress with the thin straps that I was wearing when you came to the house a few days later. The low neckline framed my neck and revealed the bones of my shoulders. My mother said that blue dress brought out the colour of my eyes. She also said that the blue was 'the colour of the Blessed Virgin'!

Anna

My mother died when I was 14. A car accident. It's been six years, and even if I'm told that I look like her I have trouble remembering her face. I look at that photo on the nightstand—she is riding, galloping, in a field on a white horse in a never-ending present. At the bottom of the armoire her old LPs are stacked upright—Bach, Schubert, Janáček, Schubert, Shostakovitch . . . next to the fireplace, in a little glass-doored bookcase, are the books she always wanted me to read—*The Red and the Black* (in a volume that had been handled so many times it is wrapped in Christofle tissue paper), *Pride and Prejudice*, *The Sorrows of Young Werther*, *Lolita* and even *Enemies, a Love Story* with a bright pink cover.

I pass my hand over the wooden headboard. As the people around here say, my mother is gone. But she left behind her young girl's bedroom. Her desk where I've put my own books (*Physiology of the Neuron, Handbook of Stroke, Peripheral Neuropathy, Semiology of the Nervous System . . .*), the mantle above the fireplace, a coat stand in front of the window looking on to the river, a metal box with pipe tobacco in it, an empty glasses case . . .

I'm fascinated by all these objects. It is only we who die, everything else remains.

Marie

When you left, I was half-naked. After the Song of Songs, knowing that I was a virgin, you said we would have to wait—wait until I was 18. We were on the threshold of love. I could have 'come to my senses' then. I didn't. I don't remember even having considered it.

Anna

There is one thing I remember clearly. She was short-sighted. She would encounter people in the street without recognizing them, and could read street signs only when she was right on top of them. She guessed at Métro stations by the general shapes of their names—Sèvres-Babylone, Alma, Trocadéro . . . a bit like when you're learning how to read.

But none of that bothered her. Except when she was driving or at the cinema, my mother never wore her glasses. It wasn't because she was vain. It was more a modus vivendi. She needed that delicate blurriness that, in the eyes of the short-sighted, envelopes everything in gauze. Nothing stands out, no sharp edges. She lived in a softened world. No unnecessary detail hindered her gaze.

'When I walk around Paris I see only what's essential,' she used to say. 'Proportions, perspectives, lines . . . Even faces seem more harmonious. Look at that woman over there, the blonde one with the green coat,' she said to me one day in the Métro. 'When I look at her, she reminds me of a Botticelli. Why would you want to "correct" that? I'm sure that if you gave me my glasses, here, now, my Botticelli would turn into a cubist head!

'No, really. We short-sighted people are very fortunate to see the world as it isn't.'

Marie

You're going to laugh. The other day, when she came home from school, my daughter Sacha, who's studying to get into ENA, had 'something to tell us'. A 'chick in her class' was going out with the philosophy teacher. He was at least 25 years older than she, but already last year he was 'really into her'. Now, they've been together for several months and the girl's just announced that she's pregnant.

My daughters were horrified—'that's disgusting'. I tried to get them to talk about it. Why were they so disgusted? Because the situation veered from the usual images of happiness? Or, on the contrary, because it fell into the stereotypes of *Manhattan* or *Diable au corps*? Was it the difference in age that shocked them? Was it the man or the girl they judged? Did they consider him immoral, selfish, too good, or not good enough for her? Did they think she was silly, a flirt or flighty? Guilty or the victim? Who was the dupe of whom? Was it the baby they felt sorry for? Or did they simply find the idea of grey hair next to blonde unacceptable?

I didn't get a clear answer, only disapproval. He was old and ugly and one of them asked how someone could 'have a thing for a dinosaur'. The others laughed.

I told myself that at least my daughters had their 'feet on the ground'. I thought of *Harold and Maude*. You know, the scene with the old English general commenting—a wonderful understatement—on the marriage of Maude, 80, with the young Harold, 'I don't think this is eh … quite normal.' I thought of the pontificating psychiatrist, 'It is … a very common neurosis, particularly in this society, whereby the male child subconsciously wishes to sleep with his mother.' And the repulsed priest, 'I would be remiss in my duties if I did not tell you that the idea of … your young, firm body commingling with withered flesh, sagging breasts and flabby buttocks makes me want to vomit.'

You can imagine I didn't launch into any sort of defence. I asked neutral questions. But I must have given something away. They occasionally reacted to my questions and, no fools they, started to suspect something. Might I once have had 'a thing' with my philosophy teacher? As they probed, they constructed a little story in which you were Heidegger and I Hannah Arendt. They didn't ask if you were a good lover. But, every once in awhile, the traitors, they snuck in a little jab, 'Was Heidegger cool?'

Anna

The little *écritoire*. It is to the right of the armoire, sitting on one of the stereo speakers.

The more I look at it, the more it looks at me. It's a polished wooden chest with copper inlay, a beautiful object, with a leather interior and a porcelain inkwell. I should ask Suzanne to give it to me . . .

I open it without thinking.

There are letters. Letters, cards, drawings, requests, begging . . . Mostly from my mother's old beaux.

Emmanuel complained of her fickleness. He signed his letter with this: 'Please draw a rabbit for me.'

Pierre wrote only of quantum mechanics, which was clearly his way of flirting.

Vincent, who was in law school, gave the long arguments of a future lawyer.

Eric gave detailed descriptions of his ENA exams.

Ariel offered to play the piano for her.

Jean-Michel proposed going skiing in the Tyrol . . .

People wrote a lot in those days.

I thought of Hadrien's last text message: 'UOK? RU coming this w/e?'

There was also:

An invitation to X's party.

An empty key ring.

A student ID card without the photo.

And two lines on blue paper:

'I'm not judging you, but I don't understand. You're starting something you won't be able to stop.'

The writing was round and neat. The note signed Stefa.

I remember a Stefa who was once my mother's best friend, before they lost touch with each other. But I don't understand what she was referring to.

Under the pile, at the back of the desk, there is a bundle of papers folded in half.

This letter is much longer and also more recent than the others.

I immediately recognize the writing.

'I turned 49 this year, maybe that's why I'm writing to you. You were 49 when we met. It's strange how old you seemed to me then, my dear H. I can tell you that now. The paradox, although I was only 17 at the time, is that I also felt beyond any age . . .'

Now I know that there really was a Heidegger.

I can't stop reading.

Heidegger. Were you leading me on a path to nowhere?

That's what everyone kept telling me.

But that wasn't the case. I 'ended up' OK, as they say.

All in all, we were 'together' for seven years.

Seven years. Together. Attached.

'I don't like that word "attachment", a friend told me recently. She reminded me of the tale 'The Dog and the Wolf', where the wolf said, aghast, 'Attached? So you don't run where you want?' For my friend, a loving relationship doesn't do well with ties, ropes, leashes, collars . . . My friend considers attachment in the sense of fixed, tied, pinned, chained . . . I like the word 'attachment'. It implies tenderness. Respect, too.

You were like a fixed point, H., an 'attached' point. I could move, leave, travel, come back, wander, fly away perhaps, but you were always there, you waited for me.

I remember that at the very beginning of our story I thought of that. I thought that one day something between you and me would fade away. And yet I didn't see us as ever being detached. I wanted the attachment to resist, like a pledge, to be proof that I hadn't made a mistake. It was also a way of saying to others, See, it wasn't just a fling. We remained 'very attached to each other for seven years'!

I was sure that our constancy would save us. That the weight of time would force their admiration—normal people like numbers.

Marie

But what made you 'attractive' to me, 'ravishing' in the sense that you had ravished, conquered, captured, enchanted me?

It all started with *The Misanthrope*. You had us study that sad comedy in your class. Did you choose it on purpose? 'Act II, Scene 1. Write it down. Study that passage for the next class . . .'

In the next class you sent me to the front of the room. I can see myself sitting at your light-coloured wooden desk. It was only an ordinary piece of furniture, a sort of beechwood box courtesy of the National Education Department, but sitting at your place was impressive. 'Miss N., are you ready? We are going to read this scene. You are Célimène, I'm Alceste . . .'

My heart was beating. The curtain lifted . . . you were at the back of the class, the book in your hand, and you were watching me. 'Are you ready?' The scene was unusual. You and I, at opposite ends of a diagonal line with 30 questioning faces between us. Thirty 'others' who separated and joined us, who were our audience. An impatient audience curious to see the curtain rise on this strange private encounter.

I need to mention something here. Some of those students—I won't say friends or pals, because I had very few friends in that class, except for Stefa—told me later that you had been secretly watching me in class for a long time, that you even blushed, which surprised me about you, given your natural authority. So it seemed that, right from the beginning of the school year, everyone had seen that you were not merely interested in how I was doing in class. As for me, I admit I really don't know. What if I hadn't 'seen' anything? I am so short-sighted . . . Is my subconscious short-sighted, too? In any case, this scene is fixed for ever in my memory. There will always be a 'before' it and an 'after' it.

But, for the moment, we were getting ready to play our roles, because it was a game. A strange sort of coded game, but a game all the same. We could indulge in anything, because we were only reading . . .

You began:

ALCESTE

Shall I speak plainly, Madam? I confess
Your conduct gives me infinite distress . . .

That sums you up well. You had a reputation for being authoritarian, a little gruff. You were in the right role—Alceste, that old cantankerous man, in love with a gorgeous 20-year-old woman.

Sooner or later I shall be forced to leave you;
And if I swore that we shall never part,
I should misread the omens of my heart.

Leave me . . .? Were you acting a scene? Was something going on between us?

Since I really didn't see anything, since I'm short-sighted, I was surprised, or pretended to be surprised.

CÉLIMÈNE

You kindly saw me home (or to the blackboard!), it
would appear,
So as to pour invectives in my ear.

ALCESTE

I've no desire to quarrel. But I deplore
Your inability to shut the door
On all these suitors who beset you so.
There's what annoys me, if you care to know.

That's it . . . You were jealous. So if you were jealous . . .

CÉLIMÈNE

Is it my fault that all these men pursue me?
Am I to blame if they're attracted to me?
And when they gently beg an audience,
Ought I to take a stick and drive them hence?

I liked to be a tease, too. All around me, in school and else-where, I had a stable of willing servants, one more eager than the next. It was crazy how they reassured me. I felt so unsure of myself. To be surrounded, asked for, flattered, was vital for me.

But I agree with Célimène on this point—taken individually, not one of them meant anything to me.

CÉLIMÈNE

That my good nature is so unconfined
Should serve to pacify your jealous mind;
Were I to smile on one, and scorn the rest,
Then you might have some cause to be distressed.

ALCESTE

Well, if I mustn't be jealous, tell me, then,
Just how I'm better treated than other men.

CÉLIMÈNE

You know you have my love. Will that not do?

I told you what you wanted to hear. I flattered you a bit, sly girl that I was.

CÉLIMÈNE

Your love for me is matchless, Sir; that's clear.

ALCESTE

Indeed, in all the world it has no peer;
Words can't describe the nature of my passion,
And no man ever loved in such a fashion.

There. You said that in your warm, husky, pipe-smoker's voice.

You lingered a bit on the *a* in 'passion'.

You worked the silences, your effects.

Curtain . . .

Our French lit. class, a bit stunned, had just witnessed your declaration first-hand!

Marie

You, Alceste, you were already quite smitten. And I was no doubt in enough of a state for that theatrical dialogue to assume snippets of truth as we continued. After that, throughout the entire school year—beyond a feeling of great complicity (from the Latin *connivere*, 'to shut one's eyes', as you had taught us)—nothing happened. But the essential had happened. You told me 'I love you' in the language of Molière. And in our own private theatre of love that would remain the 'primordial scene'. The Seal.

Anna

I wonder what Suzanne's reaction could have been. I keep thinking of what my sister said. How can you explain that? 'The young girl and the dinosaur' ?

Marie

I wasn't doing well before we met. Chronic depression. They took me to see several psychiatrists, but I secretly stayed in the darkness, fascinated by the worst. Several times I wanted to throw myself over some balcony or plunge into the river with stones in my pocket. Virginia Woolf and Sylvia Plath were my role models. No one ever knew. At school I was the perfect student—no problems. At home, no one seemed overly concerned about me.

One day—later on—I had a violent argument with my mother about you. It happened one evening. I can see myself standing on the kitchen table. A blue Formica table. I had run out of arguments—is that why I got up on that table?

To express my rage, I threw a plate on the floor. My mother slapped me. My nose was bleeding. I was happy to have blood to add to the tragic nature of the scene. I ran out of the house and disappeared into the night. My refuge—the horse shelter behind the black trees at the entrance to our property. I stayed there, inhaling the smell of manure and hay. I thought of that passage by Stig Dagerman I had written in my little notebook with a red elastic band: 'No one, no authority, no human being, has the right to make demands of me that run counter to my desire to live. For if that desire doesn't exist, then what can exist?'

Years later, my mother admitted how afraid she had been that evening, afraid that I would throw myself into the river. But the opposite was true. How could I tell them that, really, the opposite was true? Since I had been in your class, I had begun to breathe again. It was as if I had swallowed a box of 'uppers', as if everything was being illuminated with a brilliant light.

Have you ever experienced what the Americans call a 'near-death experience?' I had felt what those who experience it do—a swift easing of pain, a bright light at the end of a tunnel. But what I had before me was a view of life—a 'near-life experience'. How could I not have held out my hand to you?

Marie

Joking around about Arendt and Heidegger, one of my daughters asked how one could, at 18, 'fall in love with a dinosaur'? I said you can't explain attraction. However, to myself, I started to list my reasons.

First, there was your voice (even if I had it in my ear today, there is nothing more difficult to describe than a voice, the paths that it opens).

Thanks to you, I simultaneously discovered two continents—literature and my own body.

And ultimately, our connection had a whiff of incest that wasn't unpleasant.

Can everything be explained by the magnetism of Molière? By your voice that enchanted me—it had the tone of a cello, and I would later marry a cellist . . . But really, with what, with whom was I in love? With you, or with those intangible treasures? By removing the veil of sadness from me, you gave me an unexpected gift. Love and literature, sense and the senses. I discovered that life could be enjoyed.

Is it possible that there is a sort of gratitude in the act of loving abandonment? That one gives oneself to thank the other for a gift? A gift, counter-gift—what was the true reason for my attachment? The fact that you looked at me? The status I acquired when I became your mistress? The unique place you gave me—in my eyes and in those of others—by 'singling me out'? The pride that you gave me? The happiness at being loveable? The joy of being loved?

Obviously, all these questions frighten me. Because, if I follow this exploration to the end, I can't help but ask, 'What about *you* in all this?' A sort of vertigo comes on. What if that love had never existed?'

Marie

Your voice caressed me. In class, it brushed my neck, enveloped me in its rhythms. When you read Baudelaire's *Fleurs du mal* while looking at me, it was as if your words were hands. Word-hands that touched me lightly. Word-sounds that fluttered around me, touching my shoulders, settling on my neck. Intoxicating moments. Delicious emotions. My entire body listened.

Marie

Your voice again (but later). You were reading Homer to me, it was a ritual between us.

When I was very young I would tune my little radio to BBC. I didn't understand a thing but I was rolling on the waves of the language.

Your voice was fluid. When you read the *Odyssey* in Greek, the encounter with Nausicaa of the white shoulders, that sensation returned. I was windsurfing on the Aegean Sea.

Anna

I can't think about anything else. I must find that man.

I've looked everywhere in the blue room. Apart from that letter, there's nothing about H. Not a note, not a photo. My mother destroyed everything.

Find H. Not to know him, personally—I don't have what Thomas, a psychologist friend, calls 'scopic compulsion', the shameless desire to 'see'. No. It's about her. When they were together, she was exactly my age. I need him to tell me about her. I want to know everything about her, to follow her posthumously. Desires, doubts, sorrows, troubles. How they met, and what kind of lover she was. What she said to him when she was in his arms. And how she laughed. And how she let go of herself. My investigation will, I'm sure, reveal a lot about me. In the end, we only crossed each other's paths. I really don't know who she was.

Is he still alive?

Marie

Isn't it amazing how the people who meant so much can disappear so easily? Be lost in the world? And you don't even know if they're dead or alive?

A few years ago, my dear H., I saw an apparition. It was a strange occurrence to which, I hope, you will give me the key.

I was at a book fair, I was signing a biography I had written. Suddenly, I had the impression I saw you, there, in the line of readers who wanted me to sign their copies. Was it you? I admit seeing you was the last thing I expected. I was feverish. I asked the person standing in front of me, for the second time, 'What is your name?' Impossible to concentrate on what I was doing. Even less on what I was supposed to be writing. I saw you advancing in the line—which wasn't that long, but long enough so I could see you only indistinctly.

From the movements, the heavy gait, I told myself yes, it's you. And yet . . . what reason would you have had to be there? I hadn't told you about it. You couldn't have known that I'd written the book. Unless . . . an article? Maybe you read something and decided to come see me . . .?

I was getting more and more nervous. What would happen when you would be in front of me? Would you look at me without saying anything and ask me to write something in your copy? Would I stand up and suggest we go get coffee? Would we have anything to say to each other?

Would we become 'attached' again?

And then I came to my senses. A woman had been holding out her copy for a few seconds and was looking at me strangely. I muttered some excuse. I tried to find something to say. 'Is it for you?'

When I raised my head, you were gone. I looked for you everywhere. I couldn't believe it. It was the first time I cursed my short-sightedness.

PS 1. At a certain point, I stopped sending you my books. Subconsciously, I was still afraid of your reaction. One doesn't erase the teacher–student relationship so easily. I wanted to free myself, to live outside your judgement. It was the sign that I was cured.

PS 2. It's funny. A few months ago I was in Buenos Aires. I was doing research on Jorge Luis Borges and I did a long interview with his widow, Maria Kodama. Borges was thirty-eight years older than she. Maria told me of how they met, how, when she was a child, while reading one of his poems, she had fallen in love with his voice on the paper. And how even today, she wonders if she has, as they say, mourned the author of *Fictions*. Shortly before I left her, summoning all my courage, I asked her how she endured the way people looked at them together. She said this, which stunned me, 'You know, I'm short-sighted . . .'

Marie

I'm short-sighted . . . it's a bit like being under water—like when I open my eyes under water in a pool and try to guess what the world beyond it is like. From afar, I see shapes cut out with blunt scissors. Figures that are fuzzy and move around like in an animated Polaroid photo. Even farther away, they are only blurs. Blurs of colours and light, collages that overlap, giant pixels, infinitely enlarged, hydrangeas diffracted like sheep! When I was little—I must have been around four or five—I thought a white hydrangea bush was a bunch of sheep. That's how they figured out I couldn't see very well. The pleasure of being short-sighted—introducing the imaginary into the real. To want sheep and to see them in the back of the garden . . .

My love isn't blind, it's short-sighted.

Marie

We're at your house.

After making love, you wash me in the bathtub with a facecloth and lavender-scented soap.

You give me a snack a child would eat—toast and white honey.

Then we go into the living room. You put on a record, maybe the Sonata Arpeggione.

If your wife came in then, she'd join us. It often happened that the three of us would listen together, nodding our heads in time to the music.

We're at my house.

Standing next to the baby grand, I watch for you. When I hear the sound of the gravel, I know you are here. Your car appears between the tall pine trees at the front entrance. You never rang the doorbell for long.

In your arms, I smell leather—the jacket you're wearing, the warm sound of your words. I lead you into my room, I close the door. I put on some music. Maybe Schubert's *Death and the Maiden*.

I don't care if my sister can hear.

Anna

I need that past to get closer to her.

Am I opening a forbidden door?

Will I go blind, like Oedipus, upon discovering the too-harsh light of the truth?

Marie

My mother said this every day, 'You're wasting your youth.' After graduation, she insisted that I try to get into one of the business schools: 'It will bring you back to earth.' Now, when she talks to me, I hear her voice superimposed on that of the general accounting professor. You're wasting your youth (= you're wasting the capital of intelligence and charm that you have). What do you think all of that will bring you (= what will be the return on the investment of this interaction)? What are you really looking for (= how is that related to the long-term strategy of your business)?

My business was showing only losses (my time, my youth, my mind, my reason, common sense, and of course, my virtue). Each transaction that ended weighed down my balance sheet. As if it were necessary to pass a provision for the depreciation of stocks. Three hundred and sixty-five more days and still with H.? Do you realize that when you are 27 he will be 59? And so forth—37/69, 47/79, 57/89 . . . So maybe it was basically only a matter of numbers?

Anna

In my neurology textbook I come across an article whose key words are 'attachment' and 'emotion'. Seventeen subjects in love were given MRIs. In one experiment, they were asked to concentrate on a photo of their partner; in another, on the image of just a friend. Upon seeing the object of their love, certain areas in the brain—caudate nucleus, pallidum, anterior cingulate cortex and anterior insula—were immediately activated while others were unchanged—the amygdala, the right frontal cortex. It was noted that the unactivated zones were all related to negative feelings such as sadness, aggression, fear . . .

It was also noted that there is a hormone, oxytocin, that is called the 'molecule of attachment'.

And so?

So nothing, of course.

Marie

'You're wasting your youth.' They don't say that to a girl who is going out with a pimply kid. In reality, it never occurred to me that I was wasting my youth.

I was taking absolutely no risk.

I had erased the past. I wasn't looking into the future. For the first time, I was living in the moment without hoping for or expecting anything. Not for you to get divorced, or for you to marry me, or for us to have a child together. I wanted to be there, in the soft cradle of your arms where I was old and young at the same time.

An archaic consolation.

In *A Lover's Discourse*, Barthes describes that 'infantile embrace', before the logic of desire comes into play. We are, he says, 'in the realm of sleep, without sleeping; we are within the voluptuous infantalism of sleepiness—this is the moment for telling stories, the moment of the voice which takes me, siderates me, this is the return to the mother . . . In this companionable incest, everything is suspended—time, law, prohibition—nothing is exhausted, nothing is wanted—all desires are abolished for they seem definitively fulfilled.'

It didn't seem to me that I was wasting my youth.

Marie

Regret nothing, expect nothing. Do you remember that we often thought about that—it's amazing the number of people who live 'in the future or in the past'.

For us, there wasn't a before—that lost time when I didn't exist.

There wasn't an after—that stupid time when you might perhaps be dead.

There was only now. Now.

This unity of time gave everything a particular relief. An intensity that wouldn't have existed if the time we had together had spread out over a lifetime.

Marie

Of course, I'm lying when I say that we didn't have problems with time. 'You never bother to be on time,' you constantly said to me. 'Meeting me thirty-two years late . . . That's the real scandal!'

Anna

Bad timing. My mother arrived too late in H.'s life. Suzanne and my mother were ships passing in the night. Marie and Anna miss each other, in every sense of the term. This story is a series of delayed encounters.

Marie

Of course, I'm lying when I say that I don't have problems with time.

Time, for me, hauls away the blocks of pain.

Like a gift, you offered me this quote by Dale Carnegie: 'Today is the tomorrow you worried about yesterday.'

It has really helped me.

Marie

Beckett says that you can't talk about the true. That it is part of distress.

Tot homines quot sententiae, you would repeat in Latin class. So many people, so much advice, so many tales, so many fictions.

Maybe that's why I waited so long to approach this story.

Anna

While looking through one of her books I find this phrase scribbled in her handwriting on the copyright page: 'The narrator retains all rights, including that of lying to the reader.'

Marie

I wanted to capture with words a story that escapes reason. But what is this story? That of the mother who is writing today (while watching her own daughters falling in love)? That of Stefa, Suzanne, others? Isn't a story just that—the sum of the many ways of telling it? By putting all the scraps of the tales together, will I reconstitute something of that attraction that carried the two of us away?

The more time passes, the less I am really interested in the relationship itself. Knowing whether you were a catastrophe or the luck of my life. Knowing if it was acceptable, repugnant, ordinary, unique, moral or condemnable doesn't interest me any more.

Marie

You had set down a strict rule—no lying, no jealousy. Why did I begin this letter by talking about your wife?

I wasn't jealous. There was nothing admirable in not being jealous. The great advantage of our relationship is that it excluded all forms of competition. You were my first love, I was your last. I had a unique position. Nowhere, perhaps. But by being nowhere I escaped ordinary classification. Is that what I wanted?

I wonder about the deep insecurity of that female 'type' that is called a 'Lolita'. How many clichés about her ring false. Lolita is not just that young girl consumed by an Oedipus complex. She is a character that is so proud and so unsure of herself that she is beyond characterization.

'I am incomparable,' says Lolita. 'You see, at 18 I'm sleeping with Heidegger ...'

Regarding other women, our relationship was marvellously reassuring to me—I was (perhaps) the rival of all, but none could rival me.

At 18—you scrupulously waited until I turned 18 before we became lovers—I wasn't just a woman to be conquered for you, the 'blonde tornado' that irrupted into your marriage. I was also the one who unleashed the hatred of other women.

Do you remember? The girls in the class who, like me, had been your students, and were insanely angry at me. Why had you chosen me? Why me? Not all of them envied me, but our relationship created a chasm between us that made their own loves ordinary, boring, ridiculous. Do you remember Stefa, my best friend? Stefa sincerely tried to be supportive and even to understand. But she couldn't. There came a time when she decided she had to distance herself.

I'm not talking just about the other women—shocked, outraged, dumbfounded, angered, repulsed. I'm thinking of Suzanne—'Mrs Mother', as you called her . . . It's not very difficult to put oneself in the shoes of that pretty 42-year-old woman who discovered a man in her house who was older than she, older than her husband, 'of an inferior social class' (Suzanne *dixit*) and who calmly intended to take her daughter as his lover!

Anna

I've finally decided to ask Suzanne. I need my grandmother to tell me who Heidegger was . . . Here is what happened:

At first Suzanne pretended not to know what I was talking about. Then, after trying to redirect the conversation several times but seeing she wouldn't be able to, she sighed. What's the use? No past would bring my mother back. And especially not 'that story'.

Since I was insisting, she sat down in an armchair in front of the fireplace. For a long time, she looked at the fire, then said, 'You've really caught me off-guard . . . we'll probably still be here at 5 p.m. this evening.' Then she muttered a few words that I asked her to repeat:

'I can't shout about this type of thing,' she said, as if the subject required her to lower her voice, even when it was only the two of us in the dining room.

Then she continued:

'That was a painful time both for your mother and for me. Maybe she didn't experience it like that at the beginning, but there came a time when I had the feeling that it was a very heavy burden for her to carry.

'I sensed something was going on after she graduated. There was a letter on her dresser, a letter from a man whom I couldn't identify right away, I don't really remember, I did understand that she was involved with some man.

'How did I find out who it was? I don't remember that either. But when I found out, no doubt by asking around, I told your grandfather who said I was imagining things. That that wasn't it at all.

'And then I spoke to her directly about it.

'She didn't withhold or deny anything, she told me right away that yes, it was her literature professor—I don't know if he's still alive. Very quickly I understood that it wasn't a simple flirtation, but that their relationship was more serious and had gone further.'

Here, Suzanne laughed nervously. Then she continued:

'I was immediately furious at that man. Not at her. He must have been around 50, and I found it reprehensible that he didn't have enough self-control or morals not to go after a young girl—even if she threw herself at him. I don't know how it happened. In any case, a man of honour should not behave like that. For me it was a scandal, terrible.

'Of course, it was impossible to discuss it with your mother. She was under his spell to such a degree that, when we explained the dead-end nature of the situation, when we told her that it could only end in pain and heartache— and it did—she refused to listen. She said she didn't care at all about the age difference, that it didn't matter at all to her. And that she knew great love with an educated man—I don't mean intelligent, because I don't believe he was.

'It was his erudition, above all, that fascinated her. He cited Homer and Laforgue, introduced her to Schubert and Brahms. Maybe she had found a masculine presence that corresponded to her ideal man?'

Suzanne seemed to reflect:

'I wanted to talk to that man. He arrived casually one summer day. I remember him well—the absolute antihero. I thought he was ugly and badly dressed. He was wearing sandals with socks, he looked ridiculous . . . But he seemed very relaxed. I would have kept a very low profile if I had a young mistress who was still a minor.

'Of course, we didn't want to create a scandal. Your grandfather told me that a mature lover was no doubt better than someone wet behind the ears with no experience. In short, we had to live with it for years without ever talking about it openly. At the same time, there was something too open in that relationship, a sort of exhibitionism that repulsed me.

'Can H. come for lunch tomorrow? Can H. come for tea?' your mother asked me. 'We'll go in the little house . . .'

'I said, 'Yes, make yourself at home.' Then they came to see me. 'But Maman, there aren't any sheets in the little house!'

'We had to endure this.

'Some well-intentioned people came to tell us how dangerous it was, that his wife was in poor health, that his children were suffering.

"Do you know what they're calling your daughter?" they said. "They call her the little whore."

'You can imagine my reaction, as her mother.

'She didn't go on vacation with us any more. And when we were about to leave the house, she asked to use it, as well as the car. We always had to give in, or she would threaten to kill herself. Her father continued to say that it was nothing. That we should give in, that there was nothing to be done—always the same, always that inertia . . .'

Suzanne stopped talking, her face set, and opened the dining-room door. On the steps outside there was a pile of logs. She took the biggest one and placed it diagonally on the andirons. The bark was dry. The fire took off. She brushed off her clothes. Then she continued:

'The years went by. For her 20th birthday party we had to invite that man. Make the thing official.

'Everyone was stunned—what kind of insanity are you living in! How can you tolerate this?

'Then she left. For Paris. She came back on the weekends, since he lived in the area.

'Today, I often think that it was my resistance that soured our relationship—I mean our mother–daughter relationship. She saw me as an enemy whereas I never vetoed anything completely. I had tried to take the situation somewhat philosophically. After all, it was her life. I kept telling her that it could only turn out badly. But nothing I said had any effect.'

Marie

Your skin. Dancing together. Sometimes we waltzed in the living room of the big empty house. You would say, 'Watch out, the emperor is watching us.'

'Then what happened?'

'One day he fell ill, seriously ill. This was a few years later. She had gone to Paris, been accepted into her school, their relationship continued . . . And life continued as well, with that person who was there, always, in the background. A person whom we almost never mentioned but who seemed very present.

'Then one day she came out of her room in tears. She said that H. had had a heart attack and was dying. She spent days at his bedside. The family told me later that they were very upset when they went to see him at the hospital, to find her there, in the hallway.

'A heart attack . . . Yes, it was indeed an illness of the heart. Then he recovered, but she remained depressed, she wasn't well. She couldn't work any more. She cried. The day her sister turned 21—the sister who, on that occasion, had introduced her future husband to us—she spent the evening in her room, crying. Those were the consequences of a bad situation. She said her life was over. That she would never love any one like that again.

'How old was she then? Twent-four? Twenty-five? That made me laugh.'

Anna

On the bookshelves in the blue room are the first books my mother wrote. Three children's books on Greek and Roman mythology. She had been given a grant to write one of them, and she had gone to Aegina to work. She took me with her, I must have been eight or nine. I remember the Piraeus, the Flying Dolphins, the port where octopuses were drying out on a net.

During the day, she left me on the beach while she wrote. In the evening, I read what she had written over her shoulder. I was supposed to tell her if I understood everything, if the writing was suitable for my age, if she should change a word or another. I felt so responsible! One day, I told her that I really liked the story of Orpheus but that it was too sad. I asked, 'Can you change the ending?' She laughed, shaking her head. At the time I didn't understand why. Aren't we masters of the stories we tell?

Anna

Along with her books, there is an article she wrote on Venus, a text that appeared in a history journal:

'The festivals in honour of Venus all came under the sign of pleasure, a pleasure that could verge on license, as seen in the Adonia festival which marked the resurrection of her lover, Adonis.

Of her lover, or of one of her lovers. Because Venus happily went from one to another. The wife of Vulcan, she cheated on the god of fire with the god of war, Mars, who was nonetheless quite ugly. She had a son with him, Cupid. It was told (SAID) that Vulcan, furious at discovering her adultery, to avenge himself, surprised the lovers in the act and trapped them in a net, displaying them for public ridicule. But that fleeting shame did not prevent Venus from sharing the beds of many others, from Neptune to Mercury, from Bacchus to Adonis . . . and there were mortals, too, such as Anchises.

There was something uncontrollable in Venus that represents the entire palette of relationships of love—from the most innocent to the most unsettling, from the most chaste to the most unbridled. It is not by chance that the goddess wears at her waist a belt where what the Ancients described as "the attractions, the engaging smile, the persuasive sigh and the eloquence of her eyes" are enclosed. The belt was believed to have been so powerful that Juno borrowed it one day to rekindle the fires of Jupiter! It symbolizes the passion that clutches and the desire that grips, like a belt that is impossible to remove. This is why Lucretia speaks of the fear that Venus "catch you in her snare" and concludes that it is "easier to avoid the snares of love than to free oneself once caught".

There are many contradictions in Venus. The excesses of passion—of which the Ancients constantly showed that true wisdom indeed consisted of avoiding them—but also a sort of extreme tolerance. For the Romans, love and sexuality were "not perceived independently of other bodily practices". The "tutors" were a normal part of life. The Ancients openly conferred the sentimental and sexual initiation of young girls to men who were much older than they. What would have been barbarous was to throw them into a pasture with ignorant, impatient or inexperienced youngsters ...

In short, at 2,000 years distance, and regarding affairs of the heart, our moral interdicts would have made them laugh.'

Marie

One day I began to have doubts. Doubts because of a pair of sandals. Not ancient-style sandals. Not those thin straps that emphasize the calf muscle or the shape of the foot. No, big, ugly sandals, almost indecent for a man. It's what Barthes called alteration. The 'little tip of the nose' . . . 'Alteration,' he says, 'abrupt production, within the amorous field, of a counter-image of the loved object. According to minor incidents or tenuous features, the subject suddenly sees the good image alter and capsize.' The subject is 'de-fascinated'.

Barthes's example of this? The pages from the *Brothers Karamazov* where Ruskov is disinterred. His body is 'intact and pure', says Dostoyevski(y), but on his nose there is 'a faint trace' of decomposition. Barthes: 'In the other's perfect and "embalmed" figure (for that is the degree to which it fascinates me), I perceive suddenly a speck of corruption. This speck is a tiny one—a gesture, a word, an object, a garment, something unexpected which appears (which dawns) from a region I had never even suspected, and suddenly attaches the loved object to a *commonplace* world. Could the other be vulgar, whose elegance and originality I had so religiously hymned? Here is a gesture by which is revealed a being of another race.'

Had I caught you in flagrante delicto of bad taste? That day, with your sandals, you had crushed the 'beautiful image'. We were spending a few days in Jersey and I was ashamed of you, ashamed at what the hotel guests would see. It was as if there were a tacit agreement between us. Out in the world we could show the difference in our ages but not uncover toes . . .!

I didn't say anything to you, because you wouldn't have understood. We would have argued, you would have pointed out what a snob I was, bourgeois, petty, conventional . . . Or you would have conjured Barthes, too, and you would have, out of empathy, felt what one feels when the veil of perfection is suddenly torn or soiled. You would have measured the distance that separated our conceptions of 'distinction'. Once again, you wouldn't have understood. I would have hurt you badly.

Luckily, the weather never stays nice for long on the Anglo-Norman islands. The sandals went back into your suitcase as quickly as they had come out. As for me, I had never made the connection between feelings and shoes, but I know that something essential had, that day, almost been definitively crushed under our feet.

PS While I'm remembering that awful sandal story, look at what I found in the book I'm currently reading: 'Kawabata . . . receiving what must have been the Nobel Prize, because he stood facing the old king of Sweden . . . wearing white socks and curious-looking sandals . . . On the broad faces of the princes and princesses before him and, due to the height of the podium . . . lay an expression that could best be described as an anxious form of bewilderment.'

OK, I'll forget the sandals. You've been saved by Kawabata.

Marie

There was another type of shame—walking in front of the hotel manager on the Place du Panthéon. When Stefa was there, it was impossible to invite you to the tiny apartment we shared on rue Tournefort. So you came to get me at my school and took me to the Hôtel des Grands Hommes. I don't know if those great figures approved, but the hotel manager wasn't sympathetic. That plump little woman looked at me as if I were ill, and at you like you were a dirty old man. That's a shame. Her silent judgement and our not being able to justify ourselves. I could have told that hotel manager any sort of story based on the worst horrors of sex and money. She would have believed me. But to tell her that I loved you was unacceptable. It wasn't the sex that shocked her, it was the attachment.

In the elevator we laughed. And yet along with the pride of feeling misunderstood there was a feeling of unease, of uncleanness.

That evening, in the bathroom of the Grands Hommes, I decided to get dolled up. I remember that make-up session as a turning point in my femininity. I didn't want to overdo the rouge or the mascara—I know you detest 'painted women'. But I still had the heady feeling of stepping to the other side of the mirror, to the side of 'real women'.

That evening we went out to the Pleyel auditorium. After Schubert and more Schubert, I remember a Lutosławski in the second half. Strident and chaotic. I leant towards you, 'It's awful?' You murmured in my neck, 'It's modern!' We looked at each other and smiled. We didn't say anything but we 'heard' each other. A moment of grace that will never be erased from my memory. In the midst of dissonance, we were in harmony.

What a pity that we soon had to pass the small woman of the Grands Hommes again!

Anna

After listening to Suzanne, I immediately want to go look for *Lolita* on the bookshelf in the blue room.

'Lolita, light of my life, fire of my loins. My sin, my soul. Lo-lee-ta.'

I realize that in spite of the title and that opening line, the story is less about Lolita than Humbert Humbert (H. H.). Same thing in *The Enchanter*, that long novella from the end of the 1930s. 'How can I come to terms with myself?' asks the man who speaks from the first line. And later, 'Was it concupiscence, this torment he experienced as he consumed her with his eyes, marveling at her flushed face, at the compactness and perfection of her every movement? . . . Or else was it the anguish that always accompanied his hopeless yearning to extract something from beauty, to hold it still for an instant . . .? Why puzzle over it?'

I'm disappointed. I thought I would find the key in Nabokov's work. But I realize that if that theme—the passion of a mature man for a young girl—goes through all his work, it is always from the point of view of the man.

Torture, desire, immobile beauty . . . I'd like to mix up those words, throw them into the air so they will fall differently.

So they will illuminate her psyche. I want to understand Lolita from the inside.

Marie

Nabokov was obsessed by 12-year-old girls.

Poe married his cousin, Virginia, who was 13 when they got married.

Bellow loved only women young enough to be his students.

Gombrowicz and Rita, his wife, were 30 years apart.

Salinger and Joyce Maynard, 35.

Borges and Maria Kodama, 38.

Are writers perverts, victims, decadent, aesthetes, pornographers, eccentrics, enchanters, macho, hedonists, profiteers, sex addicts, idealists, animals, paedophiles, children, ogres, monsters, heroes, madmen . . .

And what about the women?

Marie

'One day, I will write our story,' I said to you for a laugh. Well, not entirely. I wanted to understand our attachment. Explain it to myself. Rewrite *Lolita* from the woman's point of view.

'If you write it, you will have to go to the very end,' you told me. For the first time, you gave me some advice. This time, it wasn't the professor who was speaking but the well-known writer you had become in the meantime.

'Here is what I advise—no docility, no modesty. Forget the well-raised young woman. Be immoral, presumptuous, arrogant, disagreeable. Dare to be absolutely disrespectful. And stay just as you are—delicate, narcissistic, hypersensitive, egocentric, wild, provocative. Don't fear going outside the lines. Choose life. Live life.

'And don't forget Baudelaire: "Real books are immoral. All literature comes out of sin."

'Does my advice seem paradoxical to you? Unhealthy? Look at any biography of a writer. Art is not the work of polite charmers, it is that of tragic figures. Of course, one can write novels in a different way, but . . .'

Anna

I understood that Suzanne wouldn't tell me H.'s name. I understood when she raised her eyebrows. That meant 'enough'. I wouldn't learn anything by searching into the past. She left the room, then returned a few minutes later with a notebook in her hand.

'Here ... here are a few pages I wrote at the time ... They'll give you an idea of what I was going through.' The way she closed the door put an end to our conversation.

I plunge into her small, regular and sharp handwriting.

'She was still practically a child, to her mother, at least. A butterfly coming out of its cocoon, she was blossoming, beautiful, lively, fragile. Long, blonde, silky hair falling down her back. She sometimes braided it like a little girl. Her candid blue eyes were clouded with a melancholy inherent in her age. She wasn't cuddly, refused hugs and caresses—you want to be detached when you're 18.

A good student, she excelled at her high school, rode horses, swam like a mermaid. More affectionate with horses than with humans, she had a complicit understanding of them. As people said, she was everything her parents could have wished for.

You couldn't read anything in her face. She didn't confide, well, maybe in her friends, but her friendships were rare, exclusive and choosy. In those days we felt she was preoccupied, even tormented. By chance, I came upon a letter that was lying around—on purpose? It was signed by her literature teacher. Nothing was said but it was obvious, and a woman can't be fooled . . .'

Suzanne then says how angry she was and how she saw the situation as 'a stain'. But her pen must have been running out of ink. As the paragraphs continued, the words became increasingly pale, practically unreadable. As if everything were falling apart . . . but I was able to read to the end:

'She was no longer afraid of showing herself with him, of inviting him, going out on his arm. Everyone knew that his wife was sinking into depression and that the family was shocked by their behaviour. I wanted no part of their adventure. I kept telling her about the precariousness of the situation, its immorality, the damage she was causing. What was she hoping for? I saw him as an ageing man taking the opportunity to have a final dalliance. For her, I saw only the pain to come.'

The last lines are so pale that I have a lot of trouble making them out:

'In the autumn, she didn't want to go to the mountains with us. I tried to use my authority as a parent. There was only crying, tears, breaking plates. That evening she went to hide in the stables. It was dark. We looked for her for a long time, with flashlights, at the neighbours', along the river.

Our fear that she might do something stupid finally made us give in.'

Anna

School yearbooks are good for this. I find Vincent. He is the only Vincent from that year, and I remember his note in the *écritoire*. He had learnt of my mother's death through the school newsletter. Of course he would be happy to see me and to talk to me about her, he tells me on the phone.

We meet in a brasserie in the Latin Quarter. He quickly tells me what he has been up to over the years. After university and law school, he had worked for a long time as a corporate lawyer. Then he got fed up. He wanted to switch gears and became a psychoanalyst. He had a cashmere scarf and an impish look, ready to laugh at himself at any moment.

Here's what he tells me about my mother and H.:

'I learnt about H. in a bus on the way to Acapulco. Why your mother and I were on that bus is an amazing story, and to tell it I have to go back a bit in time—sorry if the story is a bit disjointed. Yes, I have to go back to a finance class at school. She sat down next to me because she arrived late to class. I was immediately struck by her femininity. You know what I mean, her charm, the fine aura that surrounded her like light muslin.

'Right, the finance class. It was in the first trimester with Sieswieller. (If I remember all these details so well, it's because, as you'll understand, your mother was a very important part of my life. And so I've had time to relive this first encounter many times!) After that particular class, I didn't immediately have an opportunity to see her again, let's just say she could be just as fleeting as she was charming . . . until the day when I found out she was also going to spend her second year internship in Mexico and, when, against all expectations, she suggested that we travel together.

'I quickly understood. She was small, fragile, and she had been told that the country was filled with criminals and thugs! A masculine presence would be welcome. Let's just say that I was obviously going to make travelling easier . . . It wasn't very glorious, but I immediately agreed to be the guard dog, so to speak. I was already fairly smitten, you see. And so we left for Mexico. I went to Mexico City, and she went to Guadalajara, and we planned to get together on weekends to travel around the country.

'For me, the weeks were depressing, even though there was a beautiful office assistant from an Indian family, a true Mayan goddess, who seemed interested in me. No one could understand why I didn't pursue her. On the contrary, I asked the young woman to make calls for me to reserve train or bus seats for the weekends! I told her I had a French girlfriend in Guadalajara . . . Even today I can still see her misty black eyes the day when she said to me, exasperated, "Why do you ask me to help you meet up with another woman?"

'One weekend, in any event, we had planned our trip badly. At the bus station in Mexico City the bus we wanted to take was full. Considering the situation in reverse, we looked for destinations for which there were still seats available. It turned out to be Acapulco, a seven-hour ride, an excellent opportunity to catch up.

'I remember that the conversation became increasingly personal as the day went on. I also remember the exact moment when, in the setting sun, she told me that for five years she had been with a man much older than she, and that it couldn't continue, that she had to break it off, that she had to find a way to get out of it. My chivalrous side immediately emerged. I was filled with tenderness for her. She had confided her secret in me, I wanted to help her out. It was naive, romantic, completely absurd.

'And then . . . how shall I say it . . . you know how your mother was. She opened up then closed up just as quickly. She must have realized that she had confided in someone she hardly knew. Out of caution or discretion, she immediately retreated and kept her distance.

'That night, in Acapulco, we landed who knows how at the hotel . . . Paris! Or maybe it was the Eiffel Tower . . . in any case, the guy at reception told us right away that he only had one room with a double bed left. It was 1 am. We thought about the criminals haunting Acapulco. We didn't have a choice. So we decided to go ahead and stay there.

'It was hot that night. I went to bed in my underpants, while she was taking forever in the bathroom. She finally came out in blue silk Chinese-style pyjamas buttoned up to her ears. It made me laugh. She was so afraid something would happen between us. She wasn't a vamp but a woman-child. She thought being faithful to H. meant not cheating on him.

'In my opinion, and at 8,000 kilometres' distance, that old man seemed pretty inoffensive. But, obviously, I hadn't measured what for her "being *with* him" meant. What *agreeing* to be with him meant. She had told me that she had been in her final year in high school, that he had been her literature teacher, that they had started seeing each other after that year, and that he had even gone to see her parents—your grandparents—to reassure them, but they had not been very welcoming. That those last years, in fact, he had been sick, and that she had spent a lot of time between school and the hospital.

'For me, it was a magical weekend. There were confidences. And then the touching scene at the hotel. It was during that weekend that I said to myself, "She's the one." She was beautiful, intelligent, she had all the qualities— you know, I was checking off the list . . . all the boxes ticked off. In addition, she knew she had to leave that man. She knew it was a dead end. What more could I hope for? All I had to do was let time pass, quietly. I said to myself, "Show her you can be patient. That you can be chivalrous and patient."'

Marie

Today I found some old photo albums. The one from Mexico—it was a pleasure to go through it again. In one of the photos, I'm on the train with the wonderful name, El ferrocarril de Chihuahua al Pacifico. Vincent took the photo of me, sitting there in the half-darkness in the last car. A rickety car, panoramic view, canyons of red clay. I remember the rounded dome of this caboose. I also remember the scene you made when I came back from that trip. You refused to believe that I didn't sleep with him. You said it was impossible.

I kept those photos but I tore up all the ones of you. Too bad for your biographers. I burnt your letters, too. The past burns so easily.

Anna

The man with the white scarf orders two coffees then continues:

'So I was incredibly patient. During the week, in Mexico City, there was still that gorgeous Indian woman, and people still couldn't understand why I didn't go after her. But I was very much in love. I met your mother on the weekends and that was enough, I was happy . . . Happy and deathly afraid. One thing in particular frightened me. I had become aware of how ignorant I was! Up to then, I had lived without knowing whether Beethoven came after Mozart, or vice versa, and that detail meant nothing to me. But, suddenly, I realized the degree to which that sort of lapse was inconceivable to her. I became aware of my dizzying shortcomings. My abysmal ignorance . . . That makes you laugh?

'Like a madman I started catching up on my reading. I began with basic summaries, but my shame was in committing unspeakable errors . . . I admit that I later forgot everything, because my tastes run to Souchon rather than Shostakovich. But during all those weekends I made progress, I even had the impression I was marking points.

'One day, moreover, I think it was on the beach in Puerto Vallarta, I managed to kiss her. Don't smile, I'm very serious . . .

'Then, she shut down again, and told me, "When I'm with you, Vincent, I feel like I'm with a 15-year-old."

'If she only knew how little I cared about that. I had just kissed her and was holding her hand. I was dying with love. I had time ... She was pretty, intelligent, witty. Fragile, too. I called her Bebita, and for me she really was Bebita, that little girl I wanted to protect. Little and, to me, so very intelligent. And then I was crazy for her long, blonde hair. I told myself, "You don't really deserve her."

'And so I tried to surprise her, to amaze her. I remember having had an empty train car opened—you'll think we spent all our time on trains!—by bribing a Mexican conductor. I imagined she was saying to herself, "That man can have a car opened up just for me." I was pretty proud. You're pretty stupid at 22.

'Oh, sorry, I don't think I asked how old you are ...'

Marie

Bebita. Looking at those Mexico photos again I remember the nickname Vincent gave me. He wasn't wrong. In a sense I was still a baby when I became an adult. From Bebita to Lolita, I needed a transitional object. And that object was you. You were mine, from the beginning, I possessed you, I could love you, caress you, make you jealous, hurt you, pull off one of your ears like an old stuffed rabbit. But if I lost you I was lost.

Anna

'What happened next?'

'We returned to Paris. Very quickly I knew that I had lost the game. I wanted to see her again. She made dates that she constantly postponed. I started to fantasize about that H. I saw him dressed in grey, playing the cello in a very dark house. Away from everything. It's bizarre, I imagined him as being the age of my grandparents! He was old, but at the same time very powerful since he had succeeded where I had failed.

'Did I find that relationship incredible? No, because your mother had had me read Romain Gary's *Your Ticket Is No Longer Valid*. I had dissected that novel minutely and ended up understanding that what she was trying to tell me was quite simply, "I can't do anything else."

'Suddenly, I almost sympathized with their relationship. I finally saw that man as a co-traveller—you see how chivalrous I was! I understood how she could have fallen in love and above all the degree to which she was lost. I don't think I'm telling you anything you don't already know . . . She had a false strength. A surface strength and an inner abyss. There was that intellectual and artistic complicity between them—I think he became a famous writer later on . . . In short, that complicity meant that the physical aspect wasn't important any more. And, of course, impossible stories are always so romantic. There was something hopeless in all that which I really liked. Once again, I said to myself, "It's a matter of time." I imagined his life. His life without her *afterwards*. The hole.

'Why do you say she was lost?'

'Your mother was terribly foreign to people her own age. Life seemed incomprehensible to her. She was never at ease, even if she was successful—and she was successful because she wanted to appear perfect. She was brilliant, but how could she tell any one that she was lost? No one would have believed her. That was her tragedy. While she should have had a young 'first'—and, believe me, there were many around her, her dance card was always full—it was he and he alone who understood her. In the midst of that indecipherable chaos, he told her who she was. He was her 'teacher of life'. He showed her the rocks to step on as she forded the stream of her life. To cross it with the least difficulty possible thanks to beauty, music, "art which protects from the truth that kills".

'I remember that for me, at the time, he became indistinguishable from Romain Gary, himself. At 22, one can't fight Romain Gary! Even when I told myself he was old and sick, his time was up, when I remembered the tears in Acapulco, being the knight who delivered the beautiful prisoner from the Beast, I hadn't yet understood that polarity that drew her to him as strongly as her urge to leave him.

'And there's something else. As I told you, I was 22, and I simply couldn't imagine being 50 and in love with an 18-year-old girl. Today it might be different. I've often thought of that man, his classes, the day when she went to talk to him alone for the first time. I imagine what he must have felt at that precise moment. It must be incredibly intoxicating to see a young girl, 32 years younger than you, walk up . . . a girl who has just, in fact . . . you must wonder if you're imagining things. If you've heard her correctly. If you've understood. It must be exhilarating.'

Marie

I wonder if a woman can give herself to a man just for the pleasure of giving him a gift. An amazing gift.

As if she were announcing to him that he had just won the lottery.

That, yes, no mistake, he's really won.

Just to see his face then.

Just to be the one who has that power. The power to enchant a life.

Anna

'It's strange that you're asking me about all that,' says Julie. 'I was just thinking about that man a couple of days ago. Yet he had completely fallen off my radar.'

Since my mother's death I've got closer to my aunt. She sometimes invites me for tea. My mother was four years older than she. The two sisters were very different, but that doesn't keep me from feeling close to her as well as to my cousins, her sons. She asks me about my love life. 'Don't bring it up, it's a fiasco. Hadrien left without leaving. Can't stop sending me contradictory texts. I don't think he knows what he wants. Florian is obsessed with being a doctor. Let's talk about something else . . .'

I tell her that I had found an unfinished letter my mother had written, a letter addressed to a certain H. I spoke to Suzanne about it, but I'm missing some information. Who was H.? Can I get closer to my mother through him? Can she help me?

'It's strange that you bring that up . . .' she repeats. Unlike Suzanne, Julie talks to me openly about it. As if we are picking up an old conversation.

'. . . I really can't say why I started thinking about him again. In any case, it is less as a sister than as a mother that

I thought about him. I realized how very difficult all of that must have been for our parents—your grandparents. But just as wrenching for her.

'The paradox is that in seeing him again that way, "physically", I was filled with a sort of disgust. His little brown eyes behind thick glasses—like a retiree—his smelly pipe, his paunch, his nineteenth-century-style suits . . . all those things that clashed so horribly with your mother's youth and freshness . . .

'And yet that revulsion, I didn't feel it at the time. Why did it happen now, when I must be the age he was, and that type of situation might be something I want—I mean with my own students . . . (Julie teaches at the university.)

'Perhaps, I'm unconsciously putting myself in the place of the wife who learns of the existence of a nymphet . . . I wonder why he told her about that affair. On the one hand, a desire for transparency indicates a true degree of confidence. On the other, I can feel the horrible blow she must have felt. Had he had a lot of other women before that? I don't know . . .'

'That was their business. The contract that bound them. I mean H. and his wife . . . My mother couldn't do anything . . .'

Julie lights a cigarette.

'If I try to look at all that as I did back then . . . How can I say it? I was 14 when she was 18. I was listening to Santana, Chic and Supertramp. I was a teenager attracted by friends, fun, spontaneity. It was the style in the 1960s, I looked for clothes in second-hand stores, I wore Fioruccis and bandanas. And when I dreamt of love, it wasn't really an old scholar like him that I dreamt of. I told myself if he had had a Porsche, if he had been handsome and well-dressed, I might have understood. But having a relationship, a serious one, with "a geezer" was beyond me. As for her, he had transformed her—*she* had transformed herself for him, no doubt—into a young blossoming girl, pearl necklace, a nice little pin, Catholic-girl school skirt . . . all that exasperated me.'

She raises her eyebrows. The waitress brings two teapots. She continues:

'If you only knew how old he seemed to me. He wasn't any older than your father or your uncle today. Not really older than I am, either. It's a cliché, I know. But the mystery remains. When my children throw a party at the house, I still feel I'm one of their generation. I have to be reminded by your cousins who tell me as diplomatically as possible, "'You and Dad aren't really *old*, but to us you are." I'm forced to beg to be allowed to go downstairs and say hello and dance with them!'

Julie exhales smoke from her cigarette.

'Yes, when I think about it, he was exactly the age of your uncle today. Except that your uncle would never go out with an 18-year-old girl . . .'

'But that was her choice. She wanted to. Why do you think . . . ?'

'Your mother was always very unusual . . .'

'Unusual?'

'Yes. You had the feeling she was never in her place. She didn't do anything like the others did. I don't have to remind you that when she was 10 she changed her first name. She didn't speak. She would disappear at midnight into the horses' stalls and they would look for her with flashlights. She had frightening secrets she cultivated. She wrote thousands of pages that she hid and which I would have really liked to have read . . .'

'?'

'In the end, that adventure with H. was like a barrier erected between her and me. A way for her to point out to me that she was different. It was also a subject we couldn't bring up. With our four years' distance, we already didn't have much to say to each other, but how do you think we would have discussed our love life? That love story? She was walled up in her ivory tower, and seemed to be saying, "I am on another planet. Another plane." And it was true. In the circle of fire they had drawn around them, there wasn't any room for any one else.'

I begin to understand that my mother and Julie must have had more problems to resolve than I thought. I continue cautiously.

'Was it hard for you?'

'She was my older sister. I admired her. I wanted a connection, but their relationship kept me apart. She relegated me to a state of infantilism, mediocrity. I was pushed back into the shadows to make room for that guy. While she was once again standing out . . .'

I get the impression that Julie isn't telling me everything. After a brief silence, I ask the question again.

'Was that why it was so hard for you?'

She puts out her half-smoked cigarette by pressing hard on the butt.

'Now that you ask me, yes . . . it was hard going through that. Not really because of the chaos that it created in our family, but because the situation was forced on me without a word, without an explanation. To be in the first row and at the same time at the door. I hope you won't hold it against me if I tell you this about your mother, but I had the impression that she was doing it on purpose.'

I understand less and less of what she is saying. I stupidly repeat:

'That she was doing it on purpose . . .?'

'Well . . . OK. You're a young woman, now, after all, I can tell you. When our parents weren't there—they certainly couldn't always go to his place—she invited him to the house. They locked themselves in her room and listened to classical music. Despite the music, I could hear almost everything. It was a bit as if I were being forced to look through a keyhole. There's a movie about that, you know the one I'm thinking of . . . A man who forces a woman to watch sex scenes in the adjoining room through the keyhole. Or am I confusing it with *The Origin of the World* by Courbet that one watches that way, it seems . . .? I remember their arrival with great fanfare late one evening when I was already in bed, the heels clacking on the floor as if to announce the beginning of a play I was being forced to watch. And that old heart who was breathing louder than he should . . . I wondered why your mother was doing that to me.'

At my grandparents' house, Julie's room was next to the blue room. But the house is huge. I don't dare ask why she stayed in her room. I just question her with a look.

She repeats:

'Why did she do that? Like Zazie, to "stick it to" her parents and her sister. To say, perhaps, that we weren't paying enough attention to her. Like children who do naughty things when they want to attract attention to their little selves . . .'

That response is disorienting. I think again of the man with the white scarf telling me how lost she had been. And also of a psychiatry internship that I had done, a few months earlier. Look in on the patient in #207, they told me. The room was very dark. There wasn't a thing in the room, not a book. In the middle, there was a very young man, very handsome, his light eyes were staring at the ceiling.

'What happened to you?'

'Suicide attempt.'

He looked like a drowning victim who had been fished out against his will. We talked a little. Suddenly, the doctor opened the door, abruptly turned on the lights and said, 'Well...? Are we happy? Did we have our little fun...?'

Later, I learnt he was the brother of a well-known actress. Was he also being made to pay for 'having it all'?

I stop myself from asking the questions I am dying to ask, 'What was my mother like before she met H.? Had she changed after she was with him? Why had Julie pointed out at the beginning of our conversation how that experience must have been 'wrenching' for her? How did it all end? And when? A long time before she met my father? After her marriage—which had always seemed so happy to me—had H. died? Was he still alive?'

I am thinking 'and her?' but I hear myself ask Julie:

'And you?'

'Me?'

I don't really know what I am saying. It all revolves around 'how'. How did a woman find it possible to fall in love with someone a generation apart? The fact is I have in front of me a professor who is very nearly the same age as H. was at the time, and who has perhaps already felt emotions that were not that different from those of the other professor.

I'm not able to ask the question. The tea is cold. I finish the pot. I simply say:

'You mentioned your students a little earlier . . .?'

'Oh, yes . . . because it's a classic situation. To fall in love with a student who reflects back on you the admired master . . . I'm not surprised that someone can choose to embark on that sort of adventure. Authority, words, charisma—all that is required of a teacher—are ideal vectors for falling in love. I've never allowed myself to go there but, yes, I've already received flowers from a student, for example. What an ego-booster!'

'Tell me about it . . .'

'The guy had had an enormous bouquet of red roses delivered to me. In the following class I asked him, "You know what it means when you send red roses to a woman?"

And he answered, "Uh ... no? What does it mean?" I could see he wasn't lacking in finesse.

We laugh.

'And if the opportunity arose today?'

'If the opportunity arose ...? Well ... well, it seems I might be able to seize it. If the man were truly, how can I put it, tempting ... handsome, intelligent in the real sense ... Isn't 45 the age when one begins to need reassurance? Yes, I think I could talk myself into it.'

Marie

'The blonde tornado.' When you used that expression, it was to suggest that something external had carried you away. Hurricane, cyclone, tsunami—a serious and unforeseen climatic event had threatened your respectable 50-something virtue.

You would often return to that image, the irruption you could do nothing about.

That was the essence of our affair, by the way. In the end, no one could do anything about anything.

Anna

I keep thinking of what my grandfather said, as reported by Suzanne. 'He said that a first lover who was mature was no doubt better than a novice without experience.'

Was he the only one who didn't see the harm in something that everyone else saw only as a catastrophe?

Marie

Among those around me, only my father made me feel that I wasn't entirely insane.

Thanks to him, I learnt to beware of those who warned of disaster.

Before his death, my father had said something to me like, 'It is not proof of good health to be perfectly integrated into a sick society.'

Anna

My grandfather and H., I tell myself that those two 'fathers' might have changed her. Helped her to become the woman that I knew, the one who welcomed life as it was, with its bizarreness and its imperfections. 'Hopeless entrance, joyful exit.' That saying described my mother well.

Marie

Even today, 25 years later, they keep saying the same things to me, 'How awful! What a mistake!' As if for every transgression there is a psychic tax that can never be paid off. Do you understand that this must always be atoned for?

Anna

Following a shadow. A bizarre undertaking when I think about it. But I continue. Thanks to Julie, I find Stefa, my mother's ex-best friend—a privileged witness, in the first row during the last year in that high-school class. But Stefa doesn't tell me anything. She clearly doesn't want anything to do with that story. Her silences seem to say, 'Why go back to that anomaly? Are you sure you're not thinking too much about it? It's really bad to dwell on it. To dissect it too much.'

For a while I become discouraged. Then she starts talking about Victoria. She was in their class. I could still try to get in touch with her.

A week later, I meet with Victoria.

'. . . At one point we wondered if it was really true. If it wasn't some sort of bluff . . .

'Because . . . how should I put it? For us, in that class, your mother was sort of the perfect girl. First in the class, straight-laced, long hair. Just the opposite of a "nymphet". We knew she lived in a big house with horses, a river. All that seemed ideal—a bit unreal, too.

'That H. had been targeting her, that was obvious. He read her papers in class with a shaky voice. It was obvious, and predictable, perhaps. But was it reciprocal? His classes blew us away, as they say. H. had the art of the phrase, of the image that hits the nail on the head. I've always said there are two types of teachers in life, the flute-players—I'm obviously thinking of the Pied Piper of Hamelin—and the others. Those whose words are empty and those whose words are songs—a powerful music that grips and enchants you. I, who went on to study literature, can tell you that I rarely encountered a teacher as extraordinary as H.

'But yes, your mother . . . was she really in love with him? Or just confused? In class she played the little game that connected them. After the scene from *The Misanthrope*, it even seemed that he was teaching the class only for her. It was annoying. After all, H. was our literature teacher first, he was there to get us ready for the *bac*!

'So there really was something between them, but we didn't know what. She had mysterious exchanges with Stefa that I envied. The rest of the class didn't know a thing. But we gossiped. Had anything happened? Was she showing off? Did she want to get rid of the goody-two-shoes image that hung over her?

'It didn't matter . . . that story transformed the way we viewed her. We said to one another, "She's someone else. This girl has a hidden side. If she's doing that, she is surely capable of things we can't imagine." Suddenly, she was not just the best student in the class but a talented girl who also did things like that. It was amazing!

'Because you know . . . in the last year of high school you want to escape the cocoon of adolescence. When I said that I doubted their story for a while, I meant . . . I, too, had invented a lover that didn't exist. A Parisian I had met while skiing and whom I started to dream about. After the ski trip, I never saw him again, we exchanged a letter or two, but I let everyone believe that I was carrying on a torrid love affair. It was convenient that he lived far away. I pretended that I was going to join him for an event, a weekend, a party. I had created a little toolbox of lies that I worked with to impress the class.

'So then she arrives with her story. She and H. . . . You couldn't have made it up if you tried, even if you smoked a lot of grass—which we didn't do at the time . . . yes, suddenly she brought us into an impossible situation. Because our lovers were 20, not 49. And our lovers were sweating to get their degrees!

'But I continued with my little drama, so I wouldn't be left behind or appear boring. And when I think about it today, that's what I find most interesting, you see. Her story led us to invent other stories.

'In our little town we discussed that relationship ad nauseam. We talked about it, ridiculed it, condemned it, envied it, laughed about it or cursed it, but we completely deconstructed it. Only last year my own brother said to me, 'Did you know *she* was with H.?' I wondered how he could have been so out of the loop—maybe because he had done part of his studies abroad? His question, in any case, showed that people were still talking about them 30 years later!

'Yes, that's what I find fascinating. It had become the yeast for countless stories that grew out of it, knocked against one another, and themselves developed into other stories. Gradually, everything became a fiction to such a degree that I wondered where the truth had actually gone. It was as if we were in the presence of a myth.'

Anna

Freud thought that we reinvent our memories throughout our lives. Neuroscience confirms that intuition. What we remember is not the original memory but the one that it was the last time we thought about it. Memory is an act of the imagination. We recreate the past. To better dream of the future?

Marie

We were like Janus. A body with two faces, so tightly attached to each other that the knots had become impossible to undo. Neither of us wanted to.

And yet, I had decided to leave you. A ... rational decision. Had the words of others finally sunk in? Or was it the passing of time? Was it the strength of round numbers? I had just turned 25, and for a birthday present I asked you to help me. To help me leave.

There had been three phases in our story. The solitude before meeting you. The exaltation of the encounter, the second birth. Then, seven years later, another form of solitude, gnawing and insidious, even when lying next to you. The distancing of my friends, the disapproval of my family, the snickering of strangers in the Métro, the little woman of the Grands Hommes—all of these, I must admit, began to weigh on me.

Was I also looking for reassuring normalcy? For the strength of structures? 'Pigeonholed!' Barthes exclaimed, talking about Werther who was dreaming of marrying Charlotte. For Werther, the 'system' is a whole in which 'everyone has his place ... husbands and wives, lovers, trios, marginal figures as well [...]. Everyone except him.' Even more painful—everyone appeared to him 'granted a little practical and affective system of contractual liaisons'. Everyone except him.

I asked you to help me and you said yes. I could see that it was as painful for you as for me. You gave me some pretty lingerie to 'celebrate'. An absurd gift, like my decision. We left the store looking like we were leaving a funeral. Isn't it crazy being good? The store clerk was stunned.

Here, dear H., allow me to thank you once again. Because in my crazy desire to begin again—as if things were going to be the same—I had also decided to leave my job. Enough of accounting, mid- or long-term planning, the gross margins of self-financing. I wanted to write, and you took me seriously. You encouraged me to send my first article to a newspaper—a short little piece whose appearance I awaited feverishly, and which was going to have such a great impact on the rest of our story.

Marie

In order to transform my life, was it enough simply to change my way of thinking about it? That's what I tried to do with this analysis that you thought was absurd.

I said to you, 'Understand me, I don't understand myself.' You shrugged your shoulders. You didn't like psychoanalysis.

But I wanted to unravel the mystery, pick apart each one of those seven years, look at them head-on until an explanation appeared—a sign, a key. The design in the carpet.

I wanted to grasp what had happened to me. I wanted . . .

Every Thursday evening I saw Dr P. on rue Le Goff, near the Panthéon. I told him about you with some ambivalence. I had to both turn the page and keep you. Remove you like dead skin and lock you away like a treasure. Harm nothing.

I said to him, 'Tell me about my life. Explain it to me.'

He kept to his role—imperturbable, silent, enigmatic.

After awhile I understood that Dr P. would explain nothing about my life, but that he would perhaps help me to turn it into a story. A story that would hold up and help me to do the same. All is but stories . . .

Anna

'I had decided to leave you. A . . . rational decision.' Those overly simple sentences keep running through my head. Had my mother really sacrificed H. on the altar of reason? Was it enough for her to want it to act? How does one detach oneself?

I have penetrated so far into this story—the un-hoped-for prehistory of our family life—that I have to go to the end. Understand how one goes from attachment to detachment. How one gets over one's first love. Do you ever really get over it? What do you do with the remains, the crumbs, the fragments, the ragged shards? Should you bury them or let them be? What imprint do they leave? What psychic scar?

I would have so loved to ask my mother those questions while I was trying no longer to think of Hadrien. I miss her. While I'm asking all these questions, I feel like her absence is growing in me, like a tree.

A single person might be able to help me. I hadn't seen Laurent for years but I recognize him immediately. Laurent, the witness, my father's closest friend at Normale Sup, the lasting friend. He looks just as he did in my parents' wedding photos. A Casanova with bright eyes and a killer smile.

He compliments the 'young girl who has become a woman'. Then he asks me questions: 'My father, in Singapore, is he getting used to that assignment? And medical school, what year, a speciality in mind? Miss, please . . .? What will you have?'

He speaks softly and when I tell him the reason I called him, he smiles:

'How your parents met? But you must have heard it a thousand times already? No? One Thursday evening, 25 years ago . . . the school cafeteria was closed and, you know your father, always in a hurry, we decided to have dinner at the fast-food restaurant on rue Soufflot. And there, while we were waiting in line, a young woman with blue eyes walked up to him. She came very close. She was looking at the newspaper he had under his arm—I found out later she was short-sighted—then she said, "Could I look at that for a minute?"'

He played out the scene, his finger pointing, his eyes questioning. I knew that sequence of events, in fact. It's part of family legend. My mother was waiting eagerly for her article to appear and, that day, a miracle—there it was, in print, a quarter of an eighth of a column—a few lines, a few characters—but with her words, her sentences, her initials. Her very first published piece! 'I must have had an intriguing smile,' she would tell us when I was a child. 'The owner of the newspaper asked if it was about me, if I had won in the stock market, the lottery . . . In short, I had aroused his curiosity. He made me laugh. We started to talk. Bach, Brahms. Six months later we were married.'

When I was younger I liked to hear that tale. To hear it over and over. I played 'what if'. What if the cafeteria had been open that night? What if the article had appeared a week later? What I didn't know is that the shadow of H. was also there that night. H. who had read and approved the article. H. who had thus, without trying, contributed to guiding my mother towards the one who would succeed him.

What I also didn't know was that, that Thursday evening, my mother, in full mourning for H., had just left Dr P.'s office. Once again, she must have told him about the dead end in which she found herself. Her decision to get out. Her 'rational' decision. And then the absence, the gap, the loss. The trap that had closed on her. Her failed life. Her despair . . . Could she have imagined that a quarter of an hour later, at the base of Dr P.'s building, in the line at McDonalds, and with a boy three years younger than she, her world would be completely overturned?

'It was a moment of pure hypnosis,' continues Laurent. 'You know, those somewhat stupid moments, but which leave you speechless, when you think you've discovered the Other, that his tastes, his drives, his desires are exactly created to conform to your own. As if you had picked out the right piece of the puzzle on the first try. As if in the

Other there were revealed another You. What, you like Bach? I do, too. *The Prelude*? One of my favourite pieces! You're going to hear Oïstrakh on Sunday? Unbelievable! I was planning to go, too! And so on ... It was the first time I had seen love at first sight in person. The same amazement as if I had seen a shooting star or an aurora borealis ... I could almost feel the pheromones flying!'

We laugh. I wonder why he suddenly referred to that.

'I hope I haven't shattered the myth in saying that. Anyway, it doesn't take anything away from the element of chance. It had to be that day, in that place, with that newspaper!'

We laugh again.

'Shall we have a drink? Would you like something stronger?'

He explains that he believes in love-passion. That many insubstantial things, or that appear as such to us, are in truth very material. Language, thoughts—aren't they part of the body?

'When I think of your parents, I remember that their choice of words, the tone of their voices, their looks, all occurred in a formidable sensorial flux. You know that in the eighteenth century one said 'to make love' in talking about people who, without being in bed, were carrying on a gallant conversation? In point of fact, in front of my very eyes, your parents made love during their first encounter!'

He must sense I am uncomfortable. He changes the subject. 'And the medical world? What does it say about all that?' he asks. The nervous system, baths of humours, differences of potential, he thinks that all that makes our bodies even more magical. Don't I agree?

I am only half-listening. I see his white teeth and his slender hands. I don't know anything about the biology of love at first sight. I remember a course where images of the brain in love were compared to other images of brains connected to sexual desire or the euphoria of drugs. But what were the conclusions? Did that explain how a seven-year-old addiction could be swept away like that in a few minutes? Did that explain the reciprocal attraction of bodies and minds, the ebbing and flowing, gravity?

I am outside the conversation. My eyes are following his hands which are forming perfect ovals in the air. He is explaining something to me—but what? His palms are moving in rhythm with his voice. Sometimes they come together and form a little pyramid that he presses against his lips. Other times they move apart and his bright eyes sparkle as if he were describing a mysterious phenomenon. His elegant hands, I can see them again on the yellowed ivory keys of our old Pleyel. Laurent often played the piano in our house, when I was younger. He played jazz with large, wild gestures that made my sisters and me laugh.

I can feel my cheeks on fire. Is it the emotion or the effects of the mojito? I try to answer his questions on the brain, but can't. A whirlwind of contradictory signals are bombarding mine at that very moment, the moment when, catching his gaze, I see that he is staring at me and has sensed I am blushing. Could I . . .? A guy my father's age . . .? I would never have dreamt that the idea could even cross my mind.

'You're right,' he concludes, though I don't know what he is referring to. 'I'm boring you with all that. Shall we go grab a bite to eat?'

Then he does something unexpected—he taps the back of my hand with two fingers, and tilts his head waiting for my answer.

I hesitate for a moment . . . Could I . . .?

'I can't,' I hear myself say. 'I can't, I have to be somewhere . . . I'm already late.'

I get up quickly. Thanking him, I kiss him on both cheeks. Then I grab my purse and run out.

Marie

I was so afraid of the detachment. But was that all? To leave the man of my life for the man of my life had been so easy! I just had to let myself go. The force of the attraction was the same. I immediately recognized it.

My dear H., can you tell me what becomes of the first love? Is the trace it leaves unique? Does it remain lurking inside us? Is it reincarnated? Where does it go?

Anna

We turn lights off and on. That's the image that comes to me after I leave Laurent. I see a finger on a light switch. Off! Abruptly, caudate nucleus, pallidum, anterior cingulate cortex, insular cortex, plunged into darkness. The extinguishing of fires. Deactivation of the first love. Fading of desire.

Then the finger moves and everything comes back. In the line at McDonalds, once again, all the lights are green, as instantaneously as they had disappeared.

Marie

My dear H.,

I'm stopping this letter here. In starting it, did I have an intuition about something? That phone call I feared for some time, that unbearably sweet voice, I recognized them in a split second. And in that second I sensed a catastrophe.

I'm stopping this letter that you will never read. I'm going to get in my car and go to you.

Anna

I drive for hours before I finally get there. The road seems like it will never end. I go through villages with strange names, Hem, Lannoy, Veerberghen, I would have travelled across the world to meet him. Only he, I thought, will finally enable me to understand.

Words describing her bubble up in me—flirty, aware, solitary, cynical, talented, admired, lost . . . like bubbles on the surface of water, they come up from a bottomless well and I can't grasp any of them. My mother continues to elude me.

While I am driving I remember something. We were in the country. I'm helping her repair the cellar floor. Octagonal terracotta floor tiles. Some are broken and we are filling in the holes with a trowel and cement. Laughing, she says that she has just come up with a theory—The Theory of the Octagon. Like the tiles, each one of us is fixed in the paving of social life, connected to those who surround us by a single common side. Each tile sees only a segment of its neighbour.

Pensive, she follows the joints of the tiles with the tip of her trowel. I must have been 12 or 13 at the time. I couldn't understand what she was getting at. Nor how that theory would prevent us from tripping in the cellar that evening. Today, I find her idea banal. Is that what she wanted to tell me, that we only ever see one side of the octagon? That in speaking of her, Suzanne, Stefa, Laurent, were not talking about the same, whole person? 'My life? Which of my lives?' my mother would say while quoting that statement by Zweig that she liked so much. I wonder if that has anything to do with the 'so many fragments' in her letter to H.

At the roundabout in Veerberghen, I finally see a sign to the institution I am looking for. A specialized institution, since that's what they call it, specialized in ends. *Game over.* When I arrive, it must be around three in the afternoon. For me, too, the quest is almost over. When I turn off the engine, I have a moment of anxiety. As in 'Bluebeard', I am going to cross the threshold into the final room. How many myths portray this—the woman destroyed by her desire to know. Psyche approaching too close to the lamp from which a drop of oil falls on Eros and causes disaster.

I am wondering whether I should turn around when someone comes out. He is wearing a denim jacket and, on the steps of the entrance, puts on his earbuds as if he wants to separate himself as quickly as possible from what is around him. As I enter, I recognize the smell of chloride from my geriatrics rotation. All these places smell the same— cleaning solutions, creosote, urine, sweat, distress. In the background you can hear a remixed version of 'My Way'. Is there a show going on somewhere? I continue down a hallway towards the music. No one asks me anything. On the wall are pinned notes, a 'preliminary meeting for the elections of members of the commission of nursing and medical-technical care'. A man in slippers with a cap on his head also seems to be trying to find his way. Hanging from his walker is a plastic bag filled with 7-Up bottles.

Then the hallway ends in a large, darkened room. Nina Simone has stopped and a man announces the arrival on the stage, ladies and gentlemen, of a very young violinist, you might say a prodigy, Michael, Michael, how old are you?

I wonder why they are showing Anglo-Saxon variety shows here. It all seems so unreal. In front of the screen, wheelchairs are lined up. I see only backs. Humped backs. A grey, a blue, a pink one. Or rather a pink one that seems to be sleeping but which quickly straightens up. Her white hair is fixed with three ribbons, one of which, on top of her head, makes her look like a poodle. After the performance there is a *bel canto*, *Ti amo, e chiedo perdono, ricordi chi sono* . . . an Italian is pouring out his heart to an audience in purgatory. The poodle has gone back to sleep. I flee. Wouldn't it be better to just get out of here?

Anna

'What did you say . . .? With an H., right . . .? Are you a member of the family?'

'My mother could have been his daughter . . .'

I swallowed my words. The receptionist must think I am visiting my grandfather.

'Third floor, room 313,' she says, picking up the phone, exasperated, which never stops ringing.

When the elevator opens, I see a man who is being transported on a metal gurney. Restraints hold his ankles and wrists. He has blue and purple bruises on his skin. His eyes are closed but he turns his head on his pillow, left, right, as if to free himself from a dybbuk that is torturing him.

H.?

No. Through the window in the door of 313, I see a tall man who is standing and looking at the wall in front of him. I don't think he looks ill—even though he must be since he is here—and he is impressive. A mixture of timidity, anxiety and nerves seize me. A sense of absurdity, too. I, a young medical student, am here clandestinely, standing behind the door, observing unbeknownst to him an unknown octogenarian who had been my mother's lover. And, as if that weren't enough, I have brought the letter of a dead woman to someone who will probably never be able to read it!

It's not too late to leave. But I push on the handle and, on tiptoe, enter the room. He doesn't seem to see me. His gaze is fixed and without emotion. He is wearing a tweed jacket and corduroy trousers that contrast with what the other patients are wearing. His hands are also immobile, crossed in front, one over the other.

'Hello . . .' I say softly.

Since he still isn't paying any attention to me, I repeat, a bit louder:

'Hello . . . I . . . I'm . . .'

He slowly turns his head and—am I imagining it?—it seems that his dead gaze comes alive. I don't know how to begin. I am paralysed. There is a huge silence. I am about to open my mouth when I see he is about to say something.

'I've been waiting for you.'

Five notes of a cello. Five notes from the bow. Distinct. Without hesitation.

Even though I have never heard him, I recognize his voice. Its 'seriousness'. And since you perceive the music before the words, the meaning comes to me after the sound. It takes me a couple of seconds to understand.

'But . . .'

'. . . I've been waiting for you,' he says again, more intimately, in the tone of someone who doesn't like to have to repeat himself.

I understand that he thinks . . .

'I . . . I'm her daughter . . . I know I look like her, I'm told that often . . .'

But he doesn't respond. He stares at me strangely while I twist my purse in every direction. Through the soft leather I can feel the thick pack of paper folded in fourths. The letter. To break the silence, I finally take it out and hold it out to him.

'I came to bring you this . . .'

He doesn't move, and is still watching me as if he sees something behind my face.

'It's for you,' I insist, unfolding the sheets of paper. 'A letter for you . . .'

At that moment he holds out his hand to me. But not to take the papers. He points his finger at me and in a dramatic voice says:

'*We will separate.*'

'... Excuse me?'

He repeats, louder, and in the same slightly annoyed tone as earlier:

'Sooner or later I shall be forced to leave you;
And if I swore that we shall never part,
I should misread the omens of my heart.'

I don't expect that. He continues to stare at me. As if he were waiting for me to do something. I have just understood. Obviously, he is waiting for the next lines. For me to read my text.

'... I'm her daughter,' I repeat then, mechanically.

What more can I say? I am neither my mother nor Célimène, and I couldn't care less about *The Misanthrope*. At that precise moment I try to imagine what has happened to H. The course on cerebrovascular disease is spontaneously coming back to me slowly. 'Infarctus to the strategic areas responsible for dementia' ... I remember that depending on the location of the problem—limbic system, thalamus, associative cortex—the symptoms could evolve to the point of severe dementia. It seems that's what's happened to him. The bizarre word 'leucoaraiosis' floats through my head, which is obviously no help to me.

When our gazes cross, he has changed. Now his eyes are imploring. Almost begging. It is impossible not to react to such a plea. Doesn't a doctor, even a young one, always want to respond to a patient's needs? After all, the text is there, I have it in my hands. I just have to find the passage . . .

I flip through the pages, then I take a step toward H., I say with an air of reproach:

> 'You kindly saw me home, it would appear,
> So as to pour invectives in my ear.'

Once again, H. has come alive:

> 'I've no desire to quarrel. But I deplore
> Your inability to shut the door
> On all these suitors who beset you so.
> There's what annoys me, if you care to know.'

A sort of magnetism exudes from the man. As if, in saying those lines, he is reconnecting with something very old. As if literature reconnects him to himself. I continue, smiling:

> 'Is it my fault that all these men pursue me?
> Am I to blame if they're attracted to me?
> And when they gently beg an audience,
> Ought I to take a stick and drive them hence?'

It is actually pretty funny, the false ingenuity of Célimène, the game of cat and mouse . . .

Suddenly, however, I feel ill at ease. Why am I playing this game so easily? Is it really the doctor who is responding to the wishes of her patient? Or, more deeply—more perversely?—the girl who is slipping into her mother's skin to re-enact incognito the primal scene?

But H. doesn't seem upset. He continues with aplomb:

> 'Well, if I mustn't be jealous, tell me, then,
> Just how I'm better treated than other men?'

At that moment, I stop. 'You know you have my love. Will that not do?' would be too much. I can't say that. Molière, the cello, that is enough. I haven't driven all this way to . . . It is my turn to look him in the eyes. My turn to beg:

'Tell me about her . . .'

His expression changes, as if he is unbalanced. Then:

'I don't think one can spend one's life hating or being afraid . . .'

'Tell me about her . . .' I repeat more firmly.

'It was the autumn of 1803. One of the most beautiful in the first part of the century we called the Empire.'

I can't take it any more. I am on the verge of tears.

'My mother is dead . . . She's dead,' I say, emphasizing each syllable.

'That's OK ... anyway, I've stopped smoking ...'

He opens his arms. He says:

'Come ...'

I put the letter back in my purse and leave. On tiptoe.

Anna

During the drive back I finally understand. It wasn't the primal scene that had just been played out but the one that happened when my mother had come to see him.

I still have H.'s voice in my ear, repeating, 'Just how I'm better treated than other men?'

There is nothing. Nothing of him remains except a mechanical and empty voice. My mother must have left him defeated. Words that connect and reconnect, hadn't H. for so long symbolized that? Why did it have to be he who ...

I am shaken. I need to stop. I park in a turn-off at the entrance to Veerberghen. Right in front of the Welcome sign. Veerberghen. The name hadn't meant anything when I arrived. But, suddenly, I feel my heart clinch. I call Suzanne.

Yes. That's where the accident occurred.

She was going towards Paris.

They had searched the car.

No one ever knew where she was coming from.

And they never found her glasses.